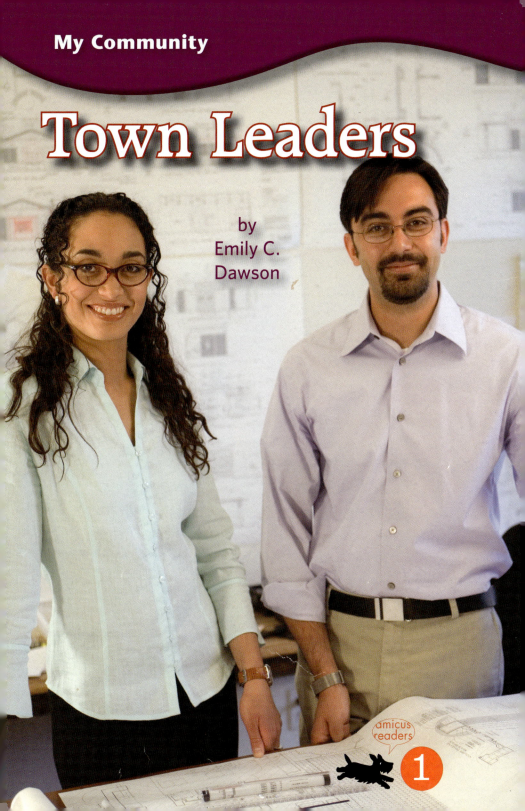

My Community

Town Leaders

by Emily C. Dawson

Amicus Readers are published by Amicus
P.O. Box 1329, Mankato, Minnesota 56002

Copyright © 2011 Amicus. International copyright reserved in all countries. No part of this book may be reproduced in any form without written permission from the publisher.

Printed in the United States of America at Corporate Graphics, North Mankato, Minnesota.

Library of Congress Cataloging-in-Publication Data
Dawson, Emily C.
  Town leaders / by Emily C. Dawson.
     p. cm. — (Amicus readers. My community)
  Includes index.
  Summary: "Describes common community helpers that a child might see around town. Includes visual literacy activity" —Provided by publisher.
  ISBN 978-1-60753-025-1 (library binding)
 1. Municipal officials and employees—United States—Juvenile literature. 2. Mayors—United States—Juvenile literature. I. Title.
  JS356.D39 2011
  352.23'2160973—dc22
                                                    2010011112

Series Editor	Rebecca Glaser
Series Designer	Mary Herrmann
Book Designer	Darren Erickson
Photo Researcher	Heather Dreisbach

Photo Credits
Amy Strycula/Alamy, 5; Corbis/Tranz, 17, 21 (paramedics); Danita Delimont/Alamy, 13, 20 (firefighter); Gaetano/CORBIS, cover; Marc Romanelli/Getty Images, 1, 11, 21 (town planner); Melissa Farlow/National Geographic Stock, 15, 21 (post master); Phil Boorman/Getty Images, 7, 20 (council, mayor); Richard Hutchings/Photolibrary, 19, 20 (librarian); Yellow Dog Productions/Getty Images, 9, 21 (police officer)

1223
42010

10 9 8 7 6 5 4 3 2 1

Contents

Who Leads a Town?	4
Picture Glossary	20
Town Leaders: A Second Look	22
Ideas for Parents and Teachers	23
Index and Web Sites	24

People in towns look after the town and help each other. What are the town leaders are doing today?

4

Mrs. Diaz is the mayor. Today she meets with the council. They talk about a new law for the town.

Mr. Gardner is a police officer. He helps keep the town safe. Today he caught someone driving too fast.

Mrs. Massa and Mr. Ramos are town planners. They tell people where to build houses and stores. Today they are planning a new mall.

Mr. Frank is a firefighter. Today there was a fire downtown. Mr. Frank helped people put out the fire.

Mrs. Evan is the postmaster. She is in charge of the post office. Today she helps Mrs. Clay send a letter to her son in the army.

Mr. Rooney leads a team of paramedics. Today a man was hurt in a car crash. The paramedics take him to the hospital.

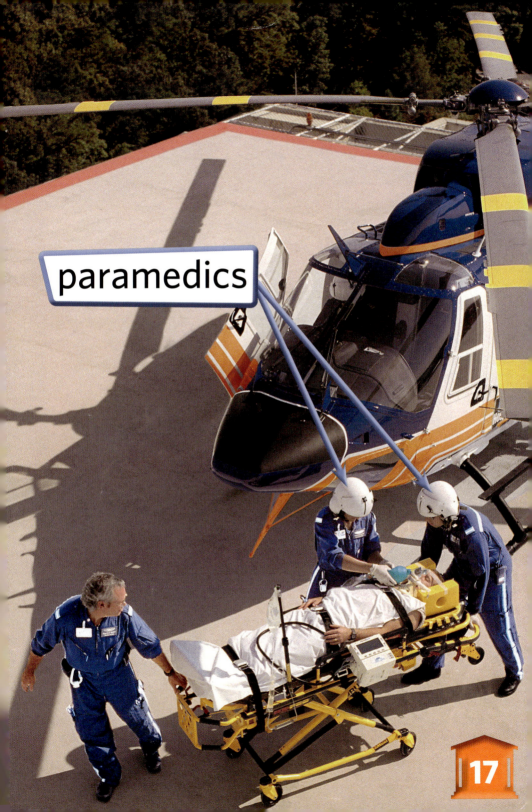

Mr. Hunt is a librarian. Today he helps Emma find books for a report. Tomorrow will be another busy day in the town.

Picture Glossary

council—a group of people chosen to make laws and decisions for a town

firefighter—a person trained to put out fires

librarian—a person who manages books and other forms of information in a library

mayor—the leader of a town

paramedic—a person trained to give emergency medical treatment

police officer—a person who keeps order in the town and makes sure laws are obeyed

postmaster—the person in charge of the post office

town planner—a person who decides where things should be built to help a town grow

Town Leaders: A Second Look

Take a second look in the book at the photos to answer these questions.

1. Which town leaders wear name tags?

2. How did the paramedics take the man to the hospital?

3. Which town leaders work in offices?

Check your answers on page 24.

Notes for Parents and Teachers

My Community, an Amicus Readers Level 1 series, provides essential support for new readers while exploring children's first frame of reference, the community. Photo labels and a picture glossary help readers connect words and images. The activity page teaches visual literacy and critical thinking skills. Use the following strategies to engage your children or students.

Before Reading
- Read the title and ask the students to suggest the people that might be in this book.
- Have the students talk about the cover photo and guess who these people are and how they might look after the town.
- Read the title page together and talk about what job these people might have.

Read the Book
- Ask the students to read the book independently.
- Provide support where necessary. Show students how to use the picture glossary if they need help with words.

After Reading
- Invite the students to return to the book and talk about the different jobs and people involved in looking after a town. Prompt them with questions, such as *What is the mayor's job? Who uses a helicopter?*
- Have the students discuss other people who help look after a town and who may not have been mentioned in the book.
- Make comparisons between the people in the book and people who look after their town.

INDEX

councils 6
firefighters 12
hospitals 16
houses 10
laws 6
librarians 18
malls 10
mayors 6
paramedics 16
police officers 8
post offices 14
postmasters 14
stores 10
town planners 10

WEB SITES

Ben's Guide (K-2): Your Neighborhood
http://bensguide.gpo.gov/k-2/neighborhood/index.html

Kids and Communities
http://www.planning.org/kidsandcommunity/

Let's Go to City Hall
http://www.hud.gov/kids/ch/ch3s_intro.html

What's My Job—People
http://www.hud.gov/kids/whatsjob.html

ANSWERS FROM PAGE 22

1. The paramedics, postmaster, and police officer
2. By helicopter
3. The mayor, council, town planners, and postmaster